DreamWorks

HOW TO TRAIN YOUR
DRAGON
2

TIME TO RACE!

Reader's
Digest
Children's Books.

New York, New York • Montréal, Québec • Bath, United Kingdom

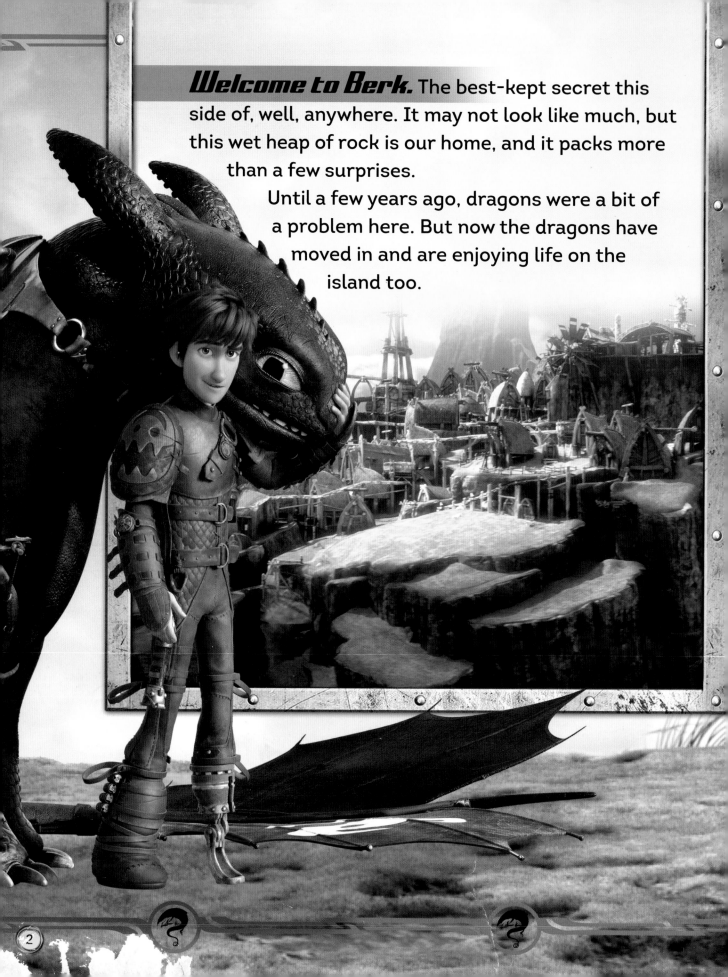

Welcome to Berk. The best-kept secret this side of, well, anywhere. It may not look like much, but this wet heap of rock is our home, and it packs more than a few surprises.

Until a few years ago, dragons were a bit of a problem here. But now the dragons have moved in and are enjoying life on the island too.

Feeding Stations

Berk now has custom dragon stables, all-you-can-eat feeding stations, and a full-service dragon wash. Because of our new neighbors, we also have top-of-the-line fire prevention!

Dragon Wash

Life on Berk is great, but not for the faint of heart. Now that dragons live here, we have a new favorite pastime...racing dragons!

Let the Races begin!

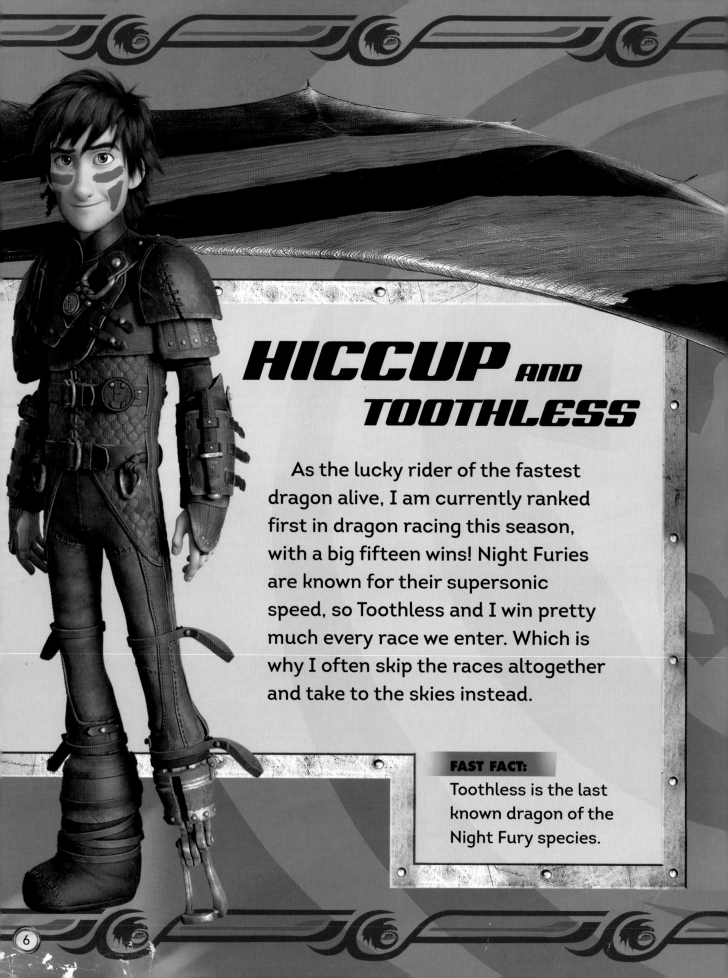

HICCUP AND TOOTHLESS

As the lucky rider of the fastest dragon alive, I am currently ranked first in dragon racing this season, with a big fifteen wins! Night Furies are known for their supersonic speed, so Toothless and I win pretty much every race we enter. Which is why I often skip the races altogether and take to the skies instead.

FAST FACT:
Toothless is the last known dragon of the Night Fury species.

TEAM STATS

HICCUP

RANK:	WINS:	POINTS:
1	**15**	**460**

AVG SPEED:
80 mph

TOOTHLESS STATS

WINGSPAN: _____ **45** ft.

LENGTH:
26 ft.

WEIGHT:
1,776 lbs.

SPECIES: Night Fury   **CLASS:** Strike

SPECIAL SKILLS:
- Supersonic speed
- Dive-bombing
- Stealth flight
- Shooting plasma blasts with pinpoint accuracy

ASTRID AND STORMFLY

Astrid and Stormfly are my biggest competition. Astrid has a knack for swooping in when the other riders least expect it. She grabs the black sheep and scores—usually for a win! And watch out for Stormfly; like all Nadders, she can shoot spines from her tail with amazing accuracy!

FAST FACT:
The Nadder breathes the hottest fire of all the dragons.

TEAM STATS

ASTRID

RANK:	WINS:	POINTS:
2	**10**	**357**

AVG SPEED:
75mph

WINGSPAN: _____ **42** ft.

LENGTH:
30 ft.

WEIGHT:
2,628 lbs.

STORMFLY STATS

SPECIES: Deadly Nadder

CLASS: Sharp

SPECIAL SKILLS:
• Shooting spines from her tail
• Great at fetching objects (especially shiny ones!)
• Incredible balance during flight

SNOTLOUT AND HOOKFANG

Snotlout is another worthy competitor. With his confidence and courage, he could easily be winning more races. But here's the thing—he's often so busy showing off that he loses focus. Luckily for Snoutlout, he rides a Monstrous Nightmare. Hookfang is brave and strong and has been known to send off a fire burst or two—even when he doesn't mean to...

FAST FACT:
The Monstrous Nightmare is as likely to attack on the ground as it is from the air.

TEAM STATS

SNOTLOUT

RANK:	WINS:	POINTS:
3	**6**	**325**

AVG SPEED:
60 mph

HOOKFANG STATS

SPECIES: Monstrous Nightmare

CLASS: Stoker

SPECIAL SKILLS:
• Bursting into flames from nose to tail
• Creating powerful wind gusts by clapping wings
• Shooting unstoppable kerosene-gel fire

WINGSPAN: _____ **68** ft.

LENGTH:
61 ft.

WEIGHT:
5,040 lbs.

FISHLEGS AND MEATLUG

Don't judge Racers by their size! Fishlegs and Meatlug may not be the most graceful racing team, but they have been known to win a race or two. Racing isn't all about speed. Strategy plays a big part. And Fishlegs is a lot smarter than he looks! If only his dragon wasn't so sleepy...

FAST FACT:
The Gronckle has been known to fall asleep while flying!

TEAM STATS

FISHLEGS

RANK:
4

WINS:
4

POINTS:
245

AVG SPEED:
55 mph

MEATLUG STATS

WINGSPAN: _____ **18** ft.

LENGTH:
14 ft.

WEIGHT:
5,724 lbs.

SPECIAL SKILLS:
• Flying backward and side to side
• Ability to hover while in flight
• Shooting flaming chunks of rock and lava

SPECIES: Gronckle
CLASS: Boulder

RUFFNUT & TUFFNUT
AND BARF & BELCH

And let's not forget the gruesome twosome! Ruffnut and Tuffnut have a couple of wins under their belts. When they work together they are unstoppable, but luckily for the other racers, they are often too busy bickering with each other to keep their heads in the game. And speaking of heads, their two-headed dragon, Barf and Belch, has a secret weapon of its own. While one head spits out gas, the other head ignites it, and...kaboom!

FAST FACT:
The Hideous Zippleback is the biggest of all dragons and has some of the smallest wings.

TEAM STATS

RUFFNUT AND TUFFNUT

RANK:	WINS:	POINTS:
5	2	280

AVG SPEED: 65 mph

BARF & BELCH STATS

WINGSPAN: _____ *38* ft.

LENGTH: *66* ft.

WEIGHT: *6,036* lbs.

SPECIES: Hideous Zippleback

CLASS: Fear

SPECIAL SKILLS:
- Twice the heads means twice the destruction
- Can transform into a flaming wheel during battle

Berk is really into dragon racing. And I'm happy to compete when I can, but adventure is in my blood, and there is so much to explore now that I am on the back of a dragon! Through my adventures with Toothless I have found my mother, Valka, and her dragon, Cloudjumper. They live at Dragon Mountain, a beautiful haven for all dragons.

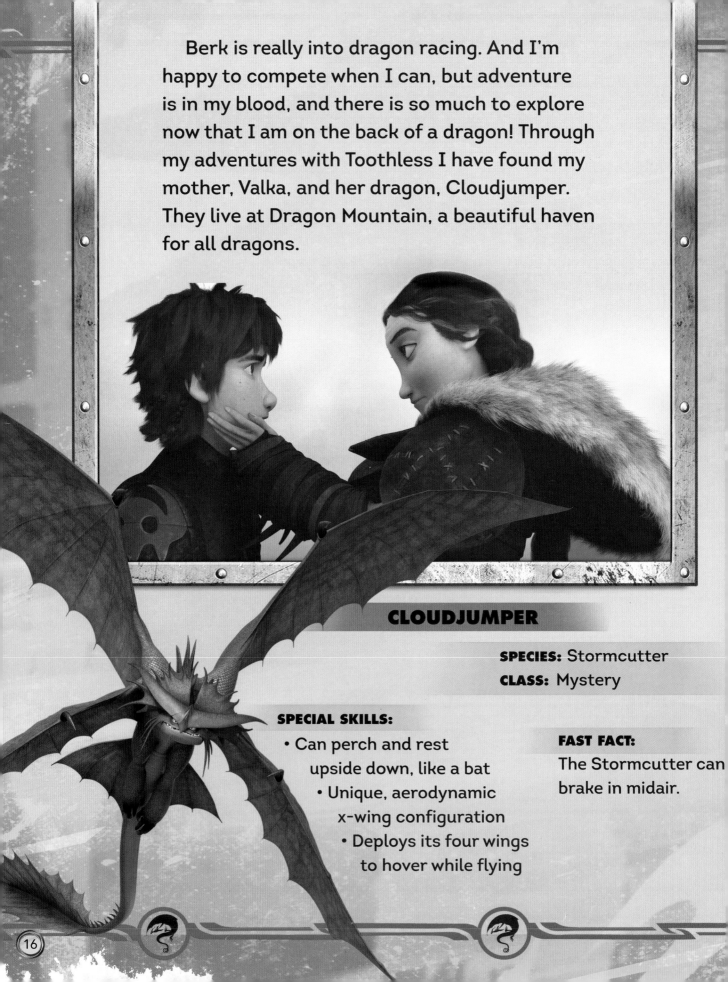

CLOUDJUMPER

SPECIES: Stormcutter
CLASS: Mystery

SPECIAL SKILLS:
- Can perch and rest upside down, like a bat
- Unique, aerodynamic x-wing configuration
- Deploys its four wings to hover while flying

FAST FACT:
The Stormcutter can brake in midair.

I should also tell you about my dad's dragon, Skullcrusher. As the chief of Berk, Stoick has taken to dragon racing like the rest of us. He doesn't race his dragon, but instead acts as race official. We Racers are happy that Skullcrusher isn't in the races—as a warrior like my dad, he'd be pretty difficult to beat!

SKULLCRUSHER

SPECIES: Rumblehorn
CLASS: Tracker

SPECIAL SKILLS:
• Headstrong and aggressive
• Armor-plated, like a rhino
• Rhino-like battering head

FAST FACT:
Rumblehorns have an excellent sense of smell.

I thought I knew a lot about dragons, but Valka has taught me even more. Every dragon has secrets, and my mom has begun to show them to me. With a simple touch along Toothless's back, Valka brought out his special dorsal blades. These aerodynamic blades allow us to soar higher and faster than ever before. Valka also revealed Meatlug's hidden ability to blast mini boulders from her skin in battle. That lug is full of surprises!

I can't wait to learn even more secrets about dragons from my mom and continue to explore the great world out there!

DRAGON ASSEMBLY

TOOTHLESS

1. Find and fold all the pieces for Toothless.

2. Fold the head weights back, and tape to secure.

3. Place the legs over the head piece. Then slide the belly through the slit.

4. Tape the leg piece to the head piece.

5. Now add the head and legs to the wing piece. Line up with the gray box as shown, and secure with tape.

6. Fold both sides of the dragon's head down, and fold the dragon in the center. Next, fold down the legs so they touch.

7. Then tape as shown.

Close-up:

tape

tape

tape

tape

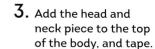

1. Find and fold all the pieces.

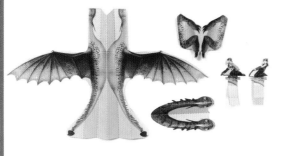

2. Fold the wings together, and tape.

3. Add the head and neck piece to the top of the body, and tape.

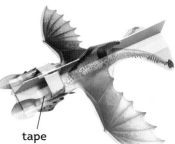

4. Add the legs to the body by lining up the art, and tape.

5. Fold the small tabs on Ruff and Tuff and insert them through the slots on the neck piece.

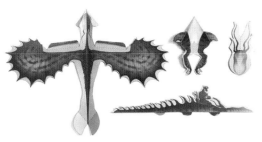

6. Tape the supports down as shown.

tape

HOOKFANG

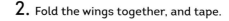
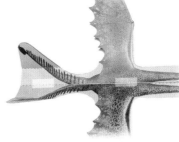

1. Find and fold all the pieces.

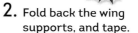

2. Fold back the wing supports, and tape.

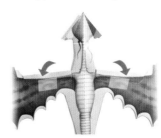

3. Tape down Snotlout on the three tabs.

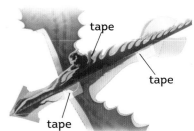

tape

tape

tape

4. Add the head piece by squeezing the neck slightly and taping down.

5. Position the legs by lining up the art, and tape them in place.

6. Make sure Snotlout is standing straight.

STORMFLY

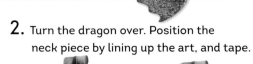

1. Find and fold all the pieces.

2. Turn the dragon over. Position the neck piece by lining up the art, and tape.

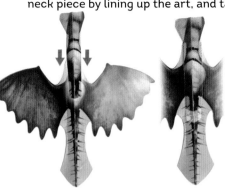

3. Add Astrid as shown and tape.

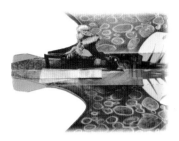

4. Squeeze the head together, and tape down the tab on the inside.

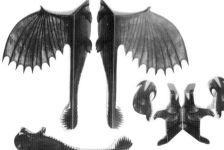

5. Slide the head over the horn. Then tape the head to the neck.

6. Position the legs by lining up the art, and tape them in place.

SKULLCRUSHER

1. Find and fold all the pieces.

2. Fold back the head weights, and fold as shown.

tape

3. Attach the wing pieces together, and tape only at the bottom.

4. Attach the head, and add the saddle piece between the wings.

5. Position the saddle piece by lining up the tail fins.

6. Then tape as shown.

tape

tape

tape

Close-up:

CLOUDJUMPER

1. Find and fold all the pieces.

2. Fold the lower wings together, and tape.

3. Insert the center piece with spikes by sliding the two tabs through the upper wings.

4. Squeeze the head together and tape down the tab on the inside.

5. Now add the upper wings to the lower wings by sliding the tabs through the lower wings, and secure.

6. Add the legs by sliding them onto the notches on the lower wings.

8. When complete, straighten the legs and make sure the wing supports are secure.

7. Then tape the folded leg piece to the upper wing as shown.